# Rhymes

# And

# Rhythm

# An Anthology of
# Poems

# Rhymes
# And
# Rhythm

# An Anthology of Poems

First Published in India in 2015 by First Step Publishing

Editorial / Sales / Marketing Office at
303-304 Garnet Nirmal Lifestyles Ph 2
Behind Nirmal Lifestyles Mall
LBS Marg Mulund West
Mumbai 400080
E-Mail:- info@firststepcorp.com
www.firststepcorp.com

ISBN: - 978-93-83306-24-4
Publisher and Managing Editor: Rohit Shetty
Branding, Marketing and Promotions by: Design Fishing
Digital Management by: First Step Corp
Typeset in Book Antique
PaperBack: ` 250
E-Book: $ 4

## Index

# <u>Sabi Shaikh</u>

We take this opportunity to introduce you to the Author of "Via Delhi – A twisted tale of Love" which is receiving an outstanding response nationwide, Sabi Shaikh. A charismatic lad who has loads of positive energy and the charm to get you addicted to his witty and unique style of writing. He hails from the city of Mumbai but has been residing in Hyderabad from the past 8 years. He holds an MBA degree in Marketing from the ICFAI University. His biggest dream in life is to write scripts for Bollywood and win the Filmfare someday. He is also an avid animal lover and a huge fan of Mother Nature. He lives his life by a quote,

"Impossible is just a word ... Means nothing." Apart from writing, Sabi enjoys watching movies, listening to music, spending time with his loved ones and sweating it out in the gym.

# I'm now afraid of the Dark...

The night is still silent and there is nothing that I can
see,
Only the shadows of your broken promises remain
all around me.
Life was once magical which is slowly losing its
spark,
I don't want to fall in love anymore for I'm now
afraid of the dark...

I wake up every morning only to find your side of
the bed empty,
My love for you is as pure as the driven snow or by
now I would have had plenty.
I still utter you name a thousand times a day... Oh if
only you could hark,
I don't want to fall in love anymore for I'm now
afraid of the dark...

My soul these days wanders in desperation to
somehow erase my tainted past,
I try really hard to forget the funny fact that we were
separated because of our caste.
All my attempts go in vain and I end up thinking
about our long winter walks in the central park,

I don't want to fall in love anymore for I'm now
afraid of the dark...

We have played the blame game for a long time now
and it's high time that we forget,
That two complete stranger who once fell in love
just pretend that they never ever met.
I know all the answers but still like a fool I live my
life besides a question mark,
I don't want to fall in love anymore for I'm now
afraid of the dark...

I am a stupid poet and decorating my poems with
your name is all that I can do,
You fell in love with the right guy for your name
will still live in my books even after you.
I know you can only call my madness so perfectly
stark,
I don't want to fall in love anymore for I'm now
afraid of the dark...

☐

# I Walk Alone...

The wounds that you have given me will fester
forever,
I have broken down but has that ever bothered you?
Never...
I should have known that your heart was made of
stone,
I am still a few miles away from my grave and those
miles I walk alone...

I wake up every morning only to find you nowhere
in sight,
The nightmares of my past still give me sleepless
nights...
I still wait for you calls ... I still keep staring at my
phone,
I am still a few miles away from my grave and those
miles I walk alone...

I search my soul everyday for a fault that I could
find,
How could I love you so much? How could I be so
blind?
It hurts to see the distance between us with time that
has grown,

I am still a few miles away from my grave and those miles I walk alone...

My world is totally messed up and I have started giving up on life,
I have quit putting in any more efforts ... I have quit putting in any more strives,
My heart is now all broken and with pain this heart still moans,
I am still a few miles away from my grave and those miles I walk alone...

My dreams are now all broken and I die every single day,
But still I'll wish you sweet dreams and that all that I can pray,
Sometimes I wish that we hadn't met and my zeal for living would not have gone,
I am still a few miles away from my grave and those miles I walk alone...

# <u>Rahul Ahuja</u>

Rahul Ahuja is from Surat located in Gujarat. His abode is his own world of imaginations. He feels that poetry is a fortuitous journey. Poetry is the only medium with which he can express his views and feelings. He is an avid reader of poetry. May it be a crumpled leaf, floating clouds or trees, he loves to capture the essence of nature in the lens, which has also inspired him to pen down his thoughts. Poetry with a slight dose of fiction is what he craves to write. Apart from this he loves to appreciate art and believes that everything around us is art and poetry. He also maintains a blog - http://canvasofpoetry.blogspot.in/

## Parting

The last leaf fell from the branch
Sun drowned faraway into the sea
Freezing mist has engulfed the pier
Waves have lost their whispers
Birds are marching towards the abode
Rains have ceased to caress the woodlands
Starless nights yearn for an embrace
Winds are unable to howl anymore
Dreams are vanishing into the labyrinth
Mornings are infected with a drunken haze
Now, butterflies don't flutter in the spring
Flowers of passion doesn't bloom in the garden
Sky is quaffing away the intoxicating ink
Words appear to be etched everywhere
Can't you see my beloved?
Even nature is writing,
A tale of our parting

☐

# Lament

Savouring the ashes of the thoughts
Charred by the flames of melancholy
Words seared the cold pages

Soaked in the blazing ink of agony
Quenching the very thirst of its existence
Quill began to bleed poetry

Immortal voices ranted from the graves
Winds carried the stains of a forgotten story
A forlorn soul drowned in tears

Silence wailed in the insomniac night
Sleep failed to reach the eyes
Winter awoke in the heart

☐

# Poetry Shall Be Born

Sky, all barren and emptied of stars
Night refused to reveal its scars
Autumn winds casted the magic spell
The last hope of the spring fell
The ocean held back the waves
Fondles which now the shore craves
Winter froze the thoughts in veins
Ink spilled on the soul, leaving stains
Chaos has engulfed the forlorn town
The king has lost his precious crown
Corpses lay scattered in the path
Walls painted with the colour of wrath
Bouquet withered away by the tomb
Humanity awaits the words to bloom
Every page seems all tattered and torn
Amidst the mayhem, poetry shall be born.

# Simran Kaur

Simran Kaur is currently studying in 12th standard has contributed her poem for the novel 'Bizarre Emotions', Aagman literary book and for various online magazines. She is sensitive and aspire to work for the society for a noble cause. She has a great passion for writing poetry and has inherited this talent from her Grandmother. According to her " Writing is best way of powerful expressions and only lucky ones are blessed with it". She can be easily read on her blog 'My Friendship' where she frequently pour down her thoughts and feelings especially about 'Nature, Love, Relations and Friendship'. Besides that she loves doing photography and cooking.

## Nature and Humans

Searching myself in nature's element
Is something I love to do everyday?
While am on my way, I miss no moment
To hold on, think and wonder
I watch people and their expressions
The fresh morning breeze, a ladder
Or better I say a escape from exertions
That I carry with myself everyday
The sheen dew droplets drenching petals
And radiance basking through trees
Those myriad birds enchanting songs
of a new day, new start and a hope
I gaze at the sky through the gaps
Between the leaves. I enjoy this moment
When a sudden strange thought occur to me
Nature and Humans both are the God's creation
Then how come one is selfless and the other
So dead selfish

☐

## Starless Sky

Below the dark starless sky she takes a breath of sigh
A void, dwelling within her may remain concealed
Layers of mist clinch vision from those moist eyes
But what about those memories that plays
endlessly?
Long ago wounded heart with scars freshen, bleeds
She searched for a lone place to unveil her real self
A crying heart that weeps quietly among the
laughter
Unable to proceed from the last ended life's chapter
The world doesn't stops for anyone then why should
life?
She closed her swollen eyes and pressed her lips in
anxiety
Swept her ever ceaseless tears. Life is all about
moving on!
When autumn transpires, the earth becomes dry and
dead
And then, spring comes with a flair to rejuvenate the
lives
Same is the life. After the storm the day shines
bright
I shouldn't be still and fragile, I will carry on with a
true smile

Life is worth to be lived and I won't let it go passive in plight.

□

# Love is all around, in the air

A few meetings to decide,
The journey of two, for lifetime,
Life plays mischievous gamble,
Two strangers now each other's rhyme.

All of sudden, two different worlds
Merge into one elate dream feathers,
Love scattered among all pertain,
Only to whom, heart promised to be together.

We seek them in nature's element,
To embellish dream cloud with love droplets,
Heart, no more loiter in the new realm,
With the ignite of amour, ice melts.

And soon, the promising day come,
The bride and groom in pair,
A mirage that happens once in a thousand,
Love is all around, in the air.

Before the world, they vow,
To be there for each other always,
Tying a divine knot so sacred,
They become better half, spring prevails.

# Sagher Manchanda

Sagher Manchanda is a promising fiction writer and has an impressive hand at writing poetry. Born in New Delhi, India, Sagher completed his schooling from St. Joseph's High School, Solapur, Maharashtra. At present, he has applied for Arts in a renowned college in Pune, where he is residing these days. During his school days, Sagher showed special interest and enthusiasm in writing imaginary or fictional essays and stories. It was after high school, when the writer-bug in him flapped his wings and led his passion of writing to a higher level. Topics viz. Life, Ethics, Suspense, Mystery and Humour are his fields of interest and being an active blogger he has written much on each of the subjects. Sagher has won the 2014 Saarang Poetry Award by IIT Madras. He is an internationally published writer, and his work has appeared in various anthologies. The specialities that his readers notice in him are varying concepts in every new story or poem and also he weaves the thread of life and lessons through each of his write-ups. This ultimately tickles the readers with uttermost excitement while reading his work. Sagher Manchanda works under the pen-name, 'Sagher' and prefers to be addressed by the same in the literary field.

# A Celebrated Wordsmith

In a Ville, devoid of literacy,
A kid to grandpa, bothered in frenzy.
He wished to get acquainted,
With essence of words, how they scented.

The old man's eyes widened,
He stared at the boy and frowned.
In the midst of farms and barns,
How did such thoughts him surround?

"Come, if you wish in real.
There are miles to travel, to a place surreal."
Thus, the bud with his elder tree,
Left for a new world, in sweet hurry.

Their journey was rhymes and anecdotes,
By grandpa, who on the lad did dote.
All the way, the little one drooled,
Who on words, could establish such rule!

He was taken to a churchyard,
In a place, Something-Upon-Avon.
Granddad showed him a grave, covered in Jasmines,
Melancholy's own resurrection.

"Here rests Chamberlain's best man,
The hero of river Thames.
To whom the precious support of king James,
Brought stupendous fame!"

Both of them bowed to the poet,
For his grand verve and verse.
Smiling with tears up there, that language's pith,
Rejuvenated, felt again like a celebrated wordsmith.

☐

## Sleep Awhile...

The dark and greasy deeds
Of an innocent yesterday,
Have camouflaged in the quiet of night-
The obscurity in the moonlight
Has given refuge to a shivering regression.
Sleep awhile,
Until a new dawn renders you might.

Your mistakes shall hobble,
Your aggressors' heads shall wobble.
The day will again bow down to your prudence,
Just let this starry stream of ongoing pass
Sleep awhile,
Until the forbidden darkness lasts.

Let bitter memories not be your lullabies,
As with a time bygone you break ties,
Barge into dreams with a smile
For a man's dreams project his heights.
The shivering cold is here to blanket you to sleep,
Sleep awhile,
And your snores shall shake this world's infirm
eyes.

# The Florist

Miles and miles away,
In the town's old isles,
I knew a florist, wretched and old,
Whose smile shone forever as gold?

Lilies, Tulips, up kept, fresh,
Roses ready to blush, in red.
You name it, and he would present
Any flower, to earn his bread.

No one-be it a debauch, gardening for art,
Or a kid buying daisies for a start,
Ever left his stall without content,
Also a thirsty bee left quenched.

I pitied the poor florist,
He never owned his own expressions,
Smiles to garden, smiles to sell,
Always: even when his son drowned in a well.

Honourable was that flower-king,
Who never used a single petal of his own?
On his own son's funeral,
Neither could he attend it.

---

For he had commitments to style,
Weddings to decorate, promises to keep,
To make the world blissful
And maintain that fresh smile.

# To Hope

I can sing wonders of that old man,
Who, on his wife's funeral,
Wrote to hope a poem
Sitting by her freshly dug grave.

Whilst the neighbours wiped their cheeks,
As they witnessed her going to bed forever,
This man, lost in deep thought,
Came up with ways to resurrect his spouse.

His parchment soaked with his own tears,
The flooding ink on wet paper,
And the flowing emotions he did savour,
Yodelled to hope a voiceless jeer.

I can sing wonders of that old man,
Who, on the saddest dawn of his life,
Plead to the sun,
To illuminate life in his dear.

Those trembling hands
With crooked lines on them,
Penned a few words
Off the straight lines on the paper.

I really must sing wonders of that old man,
Who had hope burst into tears?
As he wrote, 'Give my life to her',
And stepped into the grave, to sacrifice and depart.

# <u>Purba Chakraborty</u>

Purba Chakraborty is a content developer by profession, author by passion and a blogger by choice. She has authored two books "Walking in the streets of love and destiny" (2012) and "The Hidden Letters" (2014). Many of her short stories and poems have been published in magazines and anthologies namely "Stories for your valentine", "Fusion-A mingled flavour mocktail", "eFiction" and "Writer's Ezine".

# The Monsters in My Bed

Drained and weary
I crashed on the bed;
My limbs are weak
And my eyes are red.

How smartly I conned the world around!
With my dark aviator shades;
A smile of opulence
To camouflage the heart that bled.

No one understood my trickery
My perplexed face went unread;
The sound of my airy laughter
Ebbed down my howls instead.

But, who can rescue me now?
From the monsters in my bed;
The malicious emotions in the form of serpent
Brutally piercing me to death.

I toss and turn with pulsating heartbeat
Till rage and vengeance make me chrome red;
I wail and whimper
For all my words that ran away, unsaid.

My tears dry up as I slowly fall asleep
The rumbling emotions depart from my bed;
They cripple me, beat me and leave me insane
Yes! The monsters in my bed.

# Your first hello!

You possessed me in your first hello,
Your bewitching baritone voice
Amidst the drizzles and thunder;
Put me under a magical spell
Entirely making me yours, now I wonder.
You touched my soul at your first hello,
Your voice sounded strangely familiar
Like the one who has been soothing me in my
dreams;
If you are a reality and not a Dreamscape
Then all I want is to be yours by all means.
You arrested my heart at your first hello,
Gently putting the cuffs on my mind
Taking control over my thoughts;
You must be a wizard or a conjuror
Who else can tie me up in a hundred sentimental
knots?
You had me at your first hello,
I realized you are the one
I have been desperately waiting for;
I am filled with an insatiable longing
To soak in the allure of your voice more and more.

# The Bittersweet Evening

Sitting on the tranquil beach,
I savoured the evening sky;
The sea waves lashed my feet
Exemplifying my unsettled mind.

The mind where you reign day and night
Despite my wants, whims and wishes;
Your memories return every single time
Symbolizing the relentless sea waves.

With a sombre heart,
I scrawled your name in the sand;
Watched it glisten in the orange sun
Mirroring my eyes that gleamed with tears.

Your words and smile came alive again
In the delicacy of the bittersweet evening;
Your presence could be felt in your absence
Surpassing every ounce of rationale and logic.

The cacophony of the waves
Brutally broke all the castles in the air;
They cleaned off your name
Depicting my washed out happiness.

## Years pass by

Years pass by
Seasons fly like a breeze,
Inscribing wrinkles beneath my eyes
Turning my black hair into a sad shade of grey.

Yet the passage of time
Couldn't touch my heart
You're safe and sound there,
Unscathed by the arduous scars
Accumulated in all these years.
You live within me every second
Your name makes my heartbeat race with joy,
And your memories keep me warm in winter.
Do I live within you too?
Perhaps, I'm just a long forgotten memory.

Years pass by
Seasons fly like a breeze
I wait for a tender stroke of serendipity
To meet you once, before my eyes close forever.

# <u>Anisha Singh</u>

Anisha Singh is an aspiring writer who writes about contemporary issues and women centric stories in general. She mostly writes short stories, book reviews and also writes poems occasionally. Two of her short stories "The Lion's Grove" and "The Green Umbrella" have been published in different anthologies. She is also an active contributor at Morsels & Juices which is a platform for amateur women writers from across the globe. She holds a graduate and a post-graduate degree in English Literature. She believes that the responsibility of a writer is to write about the realities of life and bare human emotions.

# Remembrance

I look through my window
At the grey sky, with its scarlet glow
And I am instantly reminded of your
Wheatish forehead with the large dot.
The swaying branches of Pipal
In the evening breeze
Remind me of your naughty locks
That kissed your face and flew away.
I look at the rising moon
And see in it your face
Pale, care-worn with time
And running after many children.
This is how you live in me
Through shadows in nature
And through reflections and memory
Over the horizon of time.

☐

## Memories

All I have left is a carton full of memories
And a few books with old covers
And two broken metal frames
Beyond which you stand on the edge of a cliff
Your face alights with the rim of a smile.
The mad wind tussles your silky tresses
And it maddens me to see you perturbed.
I extend my hand to push your hair away
But all I can touch is a dusty glass pane
And the pangs of an old heartbreak.
No, I do not open the letters
They lie where you left them-
Folded in the middle of old Austen's.
I close the carton and tape it rather vigorously
And with it I stuff some broken memories
And old days back in the store room.

# Nehali Lalwani

Born and nurtured in Nadiad, Gujarat, Nehali
Lalwani has completed her B.com honours, Diploma
in Labour Practices and Masters of human Resource
Management. She is carefree and expressive by
nature. Pouring out her feelings via numerous
romantic poems and stories has been Nehali's forte
that makes her a zealous writer.  Her short stories
have been published in several anthologies.
 She loves writing. She believes it is fervour; an urge;
something that gives her vista to convey her
viewpoints. Her philosophy of life says that love,
though unfulfilled it never dies.

## I Love you God...

I'm caught up in this sweet chasm,
As, I'm escaping the distress of the past,
Here, I live in the fear of God; and his dignity.
I am stooped at the feet of God,

I am cuffed with fright,
All of my troubles and pains are gone.
Tears ran down my cheeks,
When he held my hand and said "Welcome at
peaks."

Every desire on gravel has gone.
It's just me and God walking on the lawn,
The colours of heaven are so radiant and fair,
His presence, his love is all I can feel in the air.

Now, all I want to do is worship my Lord.
I honestly don't deserve this award.
No one can fathom what God has planned,
I Love you God and let that be canned.

# I am Ruined.

As, I was walking across the road,
In my little black dress,
I bid my friends goodbye.
And, I saw you passing by.

I ignored when you gestured me toward
And I headed to the road.
But little did I then know,
I was never getting home.

For, a thing of beauty is no longer joy
By your hungry hounds I was cowed.
And you came up to me with that scary crowd,
Above, the clouds parted-starting a shower.

My little black dress did no good,
For you came closer with that hood.
You knew what you had to do- I went numb,
I lost in front all scums.

Your evil smile, the devil's laugh
Still is fresh as any chaff
As you leered at me as quarry,
There began my tragic story.

You pushed me onto d wall,
And your hands traced me whole,
I scratched and kicked as I was bruised,
But, Alas! I had to lose.

Ultimately, when you were done with me,
I was cold and then you flee,
Tears flowed away from my eye,
Knowing the truth reprise.

Oh! Gone is my future, now!
For, who would love me as I avow!?"
They don't know what they say,
Though, yes, I am ruined.

□

# Don't Ever Give Up!

Don't ever give up on,
What's in your trance?
Don't ever let go of,
What's in your credence?
Don't ever say the road is too tough,
And that it's better to leave.
Don't ever think that you don't matter;
As, I don't have any ratter.

Don't permit anybody tell you,
That you can't follow your dreams
There's a magic in you excess,
That no other can possess.

A quality, and warmth at a best,
That will carry you through life's tests.
There's a magic in you,
For what you are counted in those few.

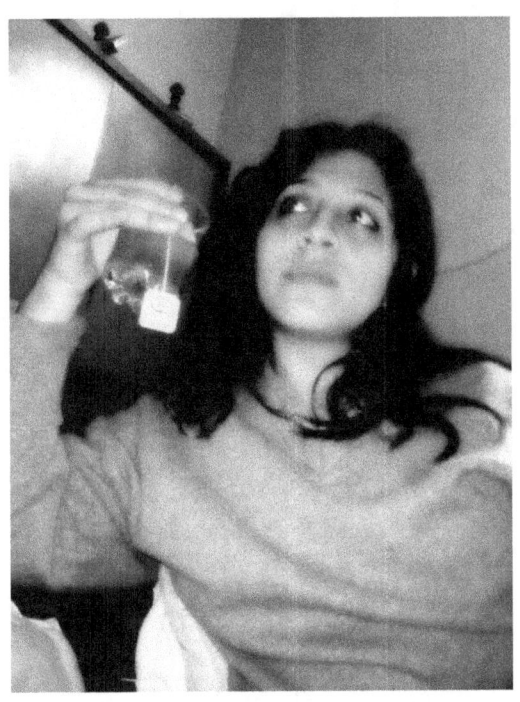

# Enakshi Johri

Active blogger and writer, Enakshi Johri, is a regular author for Indus woman writing. She is a postgraduate in Biotechnology and is an aspiring writer. She has written several articles, stories and poems and most of her content have been published in the ejournal of IWW (Indus Woman Writing). Currently, she is working as an Academic content writer with the leading firm. She has contributed in three Anthologies so far. She loves watching movies, reading books and playing basketball. She is a creative thinker and a passionate writer and loves to pour down her heart in form of words. She shares her experience and her perception through her website (http://aliveshadow.blogspot.in/).

# Tranquil memories

As the golden rays of effulgent sun fall on my face
Piercing through the thin channels between the
curtain layers
Fetching the immortal memories that I heartily
embrace
Ousting the void, thou art filling vapour.
Struggling with sleep, opening my love struck eyes
Drowning in the envelope of sublime affection
Caught unawares, how swiftly time flies
Powerless and feeble in surmounting your
addiction.
The meagre dip of your head on the soft pillow
The moist scent of your body in the ambience
All triggering the melancholy of sleeping willow
Recalling the undeniable love, not mere dalliance.
My hands, still fragrant with savoury scent of your
body
My forehead, suffused with stamps of your lips
So close, yet so distant: missing a cup of hot toddy
The plumage of memories, creating an eclipse

☐

## Weal and Woe

Pitter patter of the rain drops
Appearance of dew on the crops
Feeling the warmth of the body covering
Uneasy, anxious and unravelling
Twinkling eyes and effulgent skin
Relishing the life of the kin
Oh, what beauty!
Wondering why wouldn't life
Be easy and content
Only if difficult plights were gone
Allowing to live in an ivory tower.
With every sound of the hawk
The little heart lets out a sound of shock
Worried, perplexed and troubled about her children
As the big hawk waits with bated breath
Gathering the composed self
Wishing and praying, remembering the old elf
Her children wait and seek, she runs a risk
Their hope not shattering in the misc
Flying across like a cat on hot bricks
The little sparrow breaks the back of the beast
Eager beaver, spreading her feathers
Shielding her children, snug as a bug in a rug!

# Anuja Bhatia

Anuja Bhatia is a 20 year old girl who is pursuing English Honours. She is basically from Faridabad and loves to write poems. One of her poem has already been selected for an anthology. She aspires to become a good writer and be popular among the masses. She has a positive outlook towards life and finds her happiness in small things.

## Half of it has gone,

Half of it will still remain.
Half of my heart feels happy,
And half of it remains in pain.
Half of my feelings I display on stage,
And half of them, I captivate in a cage.
Half of what I feel is true
Half of it never felt and untrue.
Half of me want to explore the world,
And the other half wants to sit back home.
Half of my thoughts are under control,
Other uncontrollable, here and there, would just
roam.
Half of my life I have already spent,
And half of it, in future I will spend.
Half of it has been gone,
Half of it will still go on.

☐

# The Dilemma

I stand in a quandary
Of holding on
And moving on.
My heart asks to stay
But the mind just walks on.
The heart still quenches for the quest of thy love.
The eyes still haven't dried up
And feel the tribulation
Of this crying heart.
With every passing moment
Life's becoming arduous.
Bleeding, wretched heart's gruelling endeavours
Conflict with
Credos of my mind.
The crestfallen heart looks
Down the lane
To unearth the vestiges
Of thy affectionate love.
But to its astonishment,
There's none.
And I ask
Where have you disappeared?
Just vanished all of a sudden?
To leave me in a dilemma,

On this thoroughfare,
To either please
My dejected heart
Or my resolute mind!

## As long as You are a Thought

The mind,
As vast as the sky.
The heart,
As huge as an ocean.
And you,
You are a thought
As pure and pious
As ice.
As hot and burning
As fire.
You are a thought
That flies freely
in the sky of my mind.
You are a thought
That swims deep fathoms
Into the ocean of my heart.
You are a thought
That won't leave me alone
Ever!
You ain't there in person
But you,
You shall always stay with me
As long as you are a thought.

# Dilip Mohapatra

Dilip Mohapatra, a decorated Navy Veteran started writing poems since the seventies. Post His premature retirement from Indian Navy in the rank of a Commodore, he held senior leadership positions in the Tata and Suzlon groups of companies. Currently he is the Chief Mentor and Strategic Advisor to KIIT University, Bhubaneswar.

His latest poems have been featured in many literary journals of repute in India and abroad, like New English Review, Indian Review, Chiaroscuro Magazine, Helix Magazine, BlazeVox , Muse India, Statesman Festival issue, Kavya Bharati, etc. Some of his poems are included in the World Poetry Yearbooks, 2013 and 2014. He has two poetry collections to his credit, titled 'A Pinch of Sun & other poems' and 'Different Shades' published by the Authorspress India, New Delhi. He is currently working on his third project: a fiction. He lives in Pune with his wife, Tara.

## No Rhyme No Reason

I always wondered
When we curl like an embryo
And snuggle under the blanket
So peacefully
Why do the stars twinkle?
And the moon plays
Hide and seek behind
The vagabond clouds
And up in the sky
No one ever sleeps?

I always wondered
Why does ice float on water
And why do the apples fall
From the security of their boughs?
Why do waves break?
On the shores
And why do the tides turn?
Why in love we go insane
And why does hate too
Drive us to insanity?

I always wondered
When there is so much

Of symmetry and order
In the leaves on the trees
In those tiny icicles
And snowflakes
In the planets that orbit
Around some star like our sun
Why is the axis of our Earth?
Tilted and at a slant?

I no longer wonder
For that's how it ought to be.
Everything that happens
Does have fair reasons.
If the axis wasn't tilted
We wouldn't have seasons.
The blank verses
Do not take away the rhymes
The music is embedded
In their reciprocating rhythm.

□

# Let It Be

The narcissistic ocean and the sky
Rejoice and gloat over their
Reflections superimposed on each other.
Let it be.

The vagrant grey of the nimbus
Sullies the pacific blue
And the wayward waves wobble.
Let it be.

The phalanx of silver oaks across the window
Rustle and sway to the tune of an
Ambulant breeze through their branches.
Let it be.

The verdant green of the paddy field
Gets inundated by the
Slush from an overflowing gutter.
Let it be.

The halo of righteousness
Gets periodically eclipsed
By the shadow of the horns and a forked tail.
Let it be.

The ebbs and flows, the ups and downs
The blacks and whites, the cheers and tears
Resonating in an echo chamber that is life.
Let it be.

# A New Dawn

As the setting sun dissolves
On the crest of a distant hill
The lone fiddler fiddles
Under the weeping willow
On his ramshackle viola
Crying the tears of his dreams
Dictated by a distant heart
And resonating with the angst
That he had harboured
In his sobbing soul.

The viola weeps and
Its incessant tears stream
Slicing through the frozen fog
And as the woods weep
The waters weep
The winds weep

All the dead leaves and
The dried up cicadas
Are washed away
And are buried deep
In the nightly darkness
Making way

For a pristine dawn to descend
And to herald a new born sun
Once again to ride
The crest of the distant hill.

# Hitakshi Bawa

Being bubbly, carefree and full of life, Hitakshi Bawa hails from the Capital of India, New Delhi. Along with working as an Executive Administration in a MNC, she is also pursuing her MBA from AIMA. Ever since she became a self-made young woman, Hitakshi has been an avid reader, always eager to grab her favourite authors' books and leave an impressionable review. Playing with words, sharing her emotions and expressing her thoughts, gives her immense happiness. Her poems always make the readers feel good. Her short stories were published in anthologies like 'Syahi' and 'A Zest of Inklings'

Just like any other girl of her age, Hitakshi digs her moods in chocolates, balances her beautiful self on stilettos, shopping galore with friends and getting photographed from all possible angles. A down to girl at heart, rich in moral values and loyal in any relation she forms, Hitakshi unwinds her weekends at home with her small and loving family.

Connect with this beautiful, budding author with her words as she shares her ideas with you on almost every social platform like her blog @ www.hitakshibawa.com. Join her on Facebook under the name of Hitakshi Bawa and on twitter with the handle @hitakshibawa. Leave a message, discuss your ideas, take her views and be interactive with the multi-talented, enterprising and happening Hitakshi Bawa.

## Emotions Unplugged

Sometimes I feel very bad,
Sometimes I feel very sad,
Life is becoming a mess, but,
We love each other no less...

Yes I feel jealous of all,
Yes I do feel insecure,
Yes I admit it hurts me,
But reality is that it's killing me...

I'm tired of dreaming,
I'm through with trying,
My expectations are hurting me,
Tired of living, yet scared of dying...

Together we can clear the mess,
But unknowingly we are not together,
Misunderstandings or something else,
Is something really between us?

Our moments together are precious and few,
But I cherish them all more than you knew,
I love you my dear and always will do,
Stay by my side as I am nothing without you...!!

## Forever Yours…!!

My Days were without shine,
And now my nights are not being mine,
I always knew that love would find me someday,
But never knew that it would be you who will be
taking me away…

When I feel the wind, I sense your breath,
When I feel the warmth, I miss the confinement of
your arms,
When I cross a road, I yearn to hold your hand,
You've taken me over, totally and I have
surrendered myself wilfully to you…

My heart misses a beat, whenever my eyes see you,
My mind loses all its thoughts whenever I am with
you,
May be I am not good enough for you, or may you
deserve better,
But actually my love for you can face any battle…

Life is so beautiful and my life is you,
May be I don't show but I am nothing without you,
I love you so much and I mean that I do…

For now, I'll be waiting for that day when we'll be together,
That precious moment, that day when I will be all yours forever...!!

□

## Unconditional Love: Love is Life!!

Beautiful life and a beautiful love,
Is all that one always dreamed off?
All have it once for sure,
But some desire for more or some don't recognize
the pure…

Some, who get it, get pleased forever,
Heaven is on earth for them, when they both are
together,
Love is all that cherish in their souls of the world,
They do not see or feel the negativity of this world…

A treasure of love is between two hearts,
Nothing will ever torn them apart,
Their love will stood the test of time,
They will still be together as their souls entwined…

If they are together, they can conquer the world,
All the problems are meant just nothing to them,
The touch that they share,
The secrets that they hear,
Are their tender, affectionate ways…?

Getting a true one is not in everyone's fate,

And those who have it, lose it with their utmost
mistake,
If you have it, please keep it secure,
Don't let anything come between your souls…!!

# The Final Goodbye...!!

Why am I changing myself?
For whom am I waiting so while,
Things gonna change was my hope,
You'll come one day that I thought...

I treasured you in my heart,
I wished we'd never be apart,
But time wanted something else that,
I never thought I could be this sad...

I remembered the talks we had,
Yes!! I remembered the walks we made,
Still I remember you holding my hand,
But the point was that you didn't take the stand...

My heart really hurts,
My heartbeats are in pain,
As I know, life without you,
Will never be the same...

And then one day I woke up with tears in my eyes,
I told myself "that's enough" and so I realized,
That I've given everything I've ever had,

But despite all of these, you chose to break my
heart...

I can't blame you,
As you were the one I loved,
Now Wish me luck and say goodbye
As this would be the last I wished...!!

# Surbhi Thukral

Surbhi Thukral is a marketing professional turned writer. She has worked with corporations in India and the UK. After gaining success in business writing, she is determined to make a mark in the field of fiction writing. She holds Masters in Business & Management from the University of

Strathclyde, UK. She can be reached at Thukral.surbhi@gmail.com

Her work has been published in the Harvests of New Millennium, EWR: Short Stories, Taj Mahal Review, A World Rediscovered (An Anthology of Contemporary Verse), eFiction India, The Indian Trumpet, 2013 New Asian Writing Short Story Anthology, Minds@ Work 2, Seasons of Love, Fusion—A Mingled Flavour Mocktail, The Orange Frame Literary Review, Her Story: Is Not Always a Story   and Upper Cut: A Change India Initiative.

# Life

A dervish of wind
Above the flame of life.
Another existence cried,
Pervaded with terror,
Ready for the exit.
The last twist of destiny.
Life: An ephemeral comrade.
Life: A fleeting shadow.

## The Curse of Loneliness

She drowns in the forlorn
Shadow of the pale moon,
Her soul withers
On the curse of loneliness
Cast upon her fate,
She wears on her skin
The white splatter of grief,
Her heart bleeds beneath
A veil of black tears,
Echoes of dirge
Haunt her existence.

# Diwakar Pokhriyal

Diwakar Pokhriyal is a writer by passion. He has completed his engineering from NPTI Delhi & MBA from Great Lakes Institute of Energy Management Gurgaon in field of Energy. He has written 9 poetry books and 1 short story collection which are published. He has been a part of 59 anthologies/magazines with writers around the world. His works are also included in various websites. He is also a part of "Limca Book of Records

- 2015" as he participated in "Synthesis - The First book on duet poetry". He has won "Poiesis Award for Excellence in Literature-2014" for his short story. His work was selected by Aseem Ahmad Abbasi (famous lyricist) to be included in a Hindi poetry anthology. With a touch of music in him he is also a member of GRV Band as a rhythmic guitarist and song writer. The songs can be enjoyed on You tube channel of GRV Band.

## Self Destruction

Fluttering sighs can sense,
Swelling darkness,
Bamboozled entities,
Don't know what to harness,

Is that a hard question?
Worth discussing in light,
Oh my stupid human,
Your existence is in plight,

Murdered & torn apart,
Benevolent heart is a crime,
Tarnished image & polluted thoughts,
Fills the requirement of being prime,

Oh, stupid human!
Frenetic tenses are dying,
Throw away that logic,
Even your stars are now lying

Shining sun will die,
Twinkling stars will not inhale,
Earth will end in thirst,
Humanity will become a tale.

The end will be barbaric,
Of the most civilized race,
Oh lord what a satire,
They'll erase their own trace.

□

## A Fierce Warrior

I have seen her fighting,
Flawlessly and brave,
With an eye for justice,
Sending daemons to their grave,

A war of prickling words,
Or the bloodshed in lust,
The innocence may wait,
But a fierce warrior is must,

Emotional battles amongst the family,
Deadly and shining highs,
When thoughts become a dirty bed,
Who will then paint the sighs?

A war to teach the truth,
Equality shouldn't hide,
She deserves a tap on the shoulder,
She is a beautiful bride,

A war to end, fearful nights,
To welcome that shining sun,
She will now create the magic,
Leaving everybody stun

She is not just anybody,
She is shining light of the will
Even if God is against her,
She can go for a kill.

# Jitendra Pathak

Jitendra Pathak, born on 20 August. He has been pursuing B.E. in ECE stream from Dr. B.R. Ambedker University, Agra. He basically like to do poetry in both languages; Hindi and English. His genres of writing poetry are: social, romantic, religious, philosophical and sometimes it involve these all together. His view of writing says that 'writing is a part of life comes in words which has lots of experiences and more than just a thought. So, selling of these things sometimes hurts me a lot because these are not for sell, rather share them and enjoy the sheer joy of happiness. Writer don't create a story, rather, story create a writer.' He says himself a cocktail of philosophy and literature, and when you mix them together then he prepares; a poet.

## Maybe It's Her Smile

Enlightenment of moon
Make her shine
Star twinkled
Maybe it's her smile
A little darkness behind her
And she was unaware of
Where could be someone's ghostly smile?
Might harm her
Hiding it in dew
An evil essence
She smell
Move away her to the presence of darkness
And her soul crawl
Please leave us alone!
Her tears out
Shine before fall down
A body of devil
Now closer to her shadow
Her lips tremble
Like quivering of petals
Of a beautiful rose
And her sweaty skin
Like melting of snow
And splitting all over

Even over those two blossomed petals of rose
Scene was little beautiful
And little outrageous as it shows.
'Leave her alone'
A voice of an another soul
His torch of light
Pointing him a saviour
A little hard blow of his voice
Shaken his ears
Pressured his evil strength
And force him to leave
Along with those lustrous eyes
Were looking now in hurry!
Again cloudy vibe
Turns into moonlight
Which making her again shine
Star twinkled
Maybe it's her smile.

☐

# Permafrost

A night in solitude
It was like:
A desert of empty thoughts
Pain was there
And lots of doubts
Your wordless expressions
Again put me into doubts
It was like:
Deserts of punishment
And, locked in
Darkness of solitary confinement.
Breezing of sadness
And nudges
In my eyes
For a blow
And few tears of an insane flow.
Despite of being anything
I'm a case of desperation
Without you, see.
Hold me
Otherwise, I'll fall
Time is infinite
It will cover me
Beneath this sands of time

As if I'm a part of it
Like permafrost.

## Sorely At The Shore

Burning Of Lust
Melted Down
And Kiss The Dust
Air Slow Down
I Sigh
And Few Silent Words Blown
Vibe Feel
I Too Had
Sheer Love Of Heal
Print Of Some Footsteps
And Hold Few Moments
Those Moments of You and Me
I Supposed.

I Grab Them
But Wind Take Them Away
It Leave a Silence of Loneliness
And Few Tears
Those Too Get Dry
When An Unknown Soul
Blow A Breathe On It.
Bog it.

Life Stay
For A Few Moments More
Until The Moon Sail
Sorely At the Shore.

# Mandeep Kaur Heer

'Mandeep Kaur Heer' is a postgraduate in Commerce and Human Resource Management. She lives in Delhi and teaches underprivileged children. Her interest areas are Interior Decoration, Creative Economy, Guidance and Counselling, Innovation in teaching strategies, Appliqué to Spirituality and Mindfulness. She is keen to develop curriculum modules infusing art, theatre, music and poetry in

Education and done such experiments too. She writes in Hindi, English and Punjabi.

The subject areas of her writing are: life, relationships, love, romance, pedagogy, spirituality and mindfulness to humour.

She is an admirer of art and keen observer of life who finds herself penning down her thoughts. She enjoys good music, learning new things and real conversations. Nature and life inspire her. She loves rain and she loves autumn. Infact she loves every season of life.

She says "Writing to me is like rain showers on a sultry summer and sunshine in a chilly winter. It gives me a sense of free bird flying in the sky or a butterfly enjoying the beauty of a garden. Writing is my liberation, salvation and celebration."

## Kite of hope

Life may be
Rising like sun
Or may face
A downward slope.

The situation
Can be any
Do not forget
To fly
The kite of hope.

Sometimes roads can be
Wide and silky
Other times
Its walk on
A tight rope
Do not forget
To fly
The kite of hope.

Life is going to
Bring you both
Sad songs, dance
Opera, drama

Series of happy soap
Situations which you
Happily embrace
Situations which you find
Difficult to cope
Do not forget
To fly
The kite of hope.

□

## I am gonna die

Bring me flowers
I am gonna die
From ritualistic world
I wanna fly.

Bring me Jasmine
Bring me Rose
Come sooner
My eyes
**Gonna close.**

Bring me flowers
I am gonna die
Lying in my grave
I wanna see
Whose eyes are
Full of tears
Whose eyes are?
Still dry.

Bring me Olive branch
Let's end every fight
I am gonna sleep forever
I'll be no more

Tomorrow night.

Bring me flowers
I am gonna die
I wanna see
Who will rush to me?
Who with staggering steps
Still has to try

I am tired
Of laughing
Today I wanna cry
Who will kiss?
My wounds
Who is still shy?

Bring me flowers
I am gonna die
I wanna see
Who bereaves
My death
Who pounce upon
My possessions
Saying mine and my.

Bring me flowers

I am gonna die
Lets grave bring
My sleepless soul
Some rest, some relief
A peaceful sigh.

Bring me flowers
I am gonna die.

# Manaswita Ghosh

Manaswita Ghosh is a journalist and works with The Telegraph Calcutta. She is a writer, poet and an editor. Penguin Books India, British Council and Talent Flush Creations have published her in the past. Her interests include reading books and travelling.

## "A land where chains don't bind"

Those dusty evenings that brim up with life,
In an unseen land, beyond threads of time,
Call me when you feel my absence,
I shall follow you without pretence,

No excuses hold me here,
In this land where hopes are rare,
I can do with your illusions for a while,
Your dusty air and sun for this life,

Darkness doesn't bind me anymore,
Nor the heights or the sea,
For loneliness knows no bounds,
In these lands forsaken by thee,

Dear hope, your elusive land is free,
Your chains of freedom are acceptable to me,
So claim me, call me, when you feel my absence,
I shall follow you to your land - without pretence.

## "My selfish treasurer"

Yes, I found you.
Among a thousand aromas
That clung to me one night.
I found you in those darkened stars,
Full of the ecstasy of your love.
When your arms told me my horizons,
And the heart spoke of a universe so vast,
Your love - the selfish treasurer of me,
The limits of whom are lost, no, they perhaps don't
last.

Your eyes - the adventurers out at sea,
For mine have forsaken the depths.
Your dreams that wove their way out of you,
To entangle with mine, my senses.
The loves that is, like old roses in a book,
To hold and to feel, like the past, my memories to
me.
The lusted love that lasted years, a love so true and
so vast,
Your love - the selfish treasurer of us,
The limits of whom are lost, no, no limits now last.

# Jonali Karmarkar

Jonali Karmakar is a post graduate in English Literature from Indira Gandhi National Open University. She developed a penchant for writing early in her student life. She is a multilingual poet, writer and editor. She loves to escape into the worlds she creates. Everything that she writes becomes a part of her and she wants her readers to know the woman behind those words. Her work has been published in international anthologies and e-zines.

She can be reached at: karmakarjonali@gmail.com

# Moment

It comes with the sudden gust of wind —
One minute here; the next, evanesced.
We look at it, though, fail to recognize:
It's moment.
A moment of happiness
And a moment of sadness.
A romantic moment; a pathetic moment.
A moment of love
And a moment of death.
Just a flip of an eye
Just a beat of the heart —
It is gone.
The moment when I saw you,
The moment when you loved me,
Those were the moments to cherish.
Agonizing moments were those
When you walked out on me.
Those were moments of tears.
Alas! Moments are so short.
But like joss stick they burn
Like sandal, they leave an aroma.
Ah moments! Lovely moments —
Moments when I am with you:
Those are moments of eternity.

# Raw War

Give to me the life I deserve
Give to me my happiness.

Give to me the days of glory
Give to me my freedom.

Give back to me my soul of gold
And the soil fertile.

Silence is all ye are giving to me
Silent thou are to thy mother.

O! Ye war!
Ye mocker of peace
Stealthily ye rob my soul.

Whimpering of the mothers;
Whining of the orphans;
Howls of the widows;
And the dying cries of the dead —
Is all ye hold in your bosom?

Stripping from me food and shelter
Wounding my warrior sons

Stop, o you phantom
Ye monster, now stop.

The pain stifles the sound of trumpet
Yet ye blow on and on.
Red blood ye drink
Though no lamia you are
And bones ye crack to your tune.

No cause there is of your being
No reason for your felony.
Why then thou persist?
Why then your presence?

Take away the havocs ye cause
And give to me my peace.
Strike down thy raw feint
And give to me my bliss.

# <u>Ravouf Jan</u>

Ravouf is a teacher by profession and a writer by heart. She writes in English as well as in Urdu, scribbles whatever comes to her mind and whenever her hearts tells her to do so. She loves to play with the words and sometimes they say a poem or sometimes run random to tell a short story
She believes writing is the best form of self expression and by doing so a writer elates manifold.

**<u>Stone City</u>**

We live in a stone city,
Where flowers are forbidden
And fragrance is fatal!
The sky is no blue,
And the sun has a black hue.
It rains pebbles here and
Solid is dew…
Water tastes hard
And air is coloured too.
It's a new world now
A wired one, a concrete zoo!
Here adulteration is adored,
And we practice paranoid!
The rivers flow glass
And the trees hold brass…
There's a standstill,
An everlasting pause!
We live in a stone city
Where air is coloured too,
& Sky is no blue!

□

## I Retire To Write

A pen in my hand,
Refuses to write…
No, I won't run blind,
I won't tout!
People have been
Fooled by me for a long now,
Tousled in the sky
Trans myriad.
The grip I let it loose
No more, I won't choose…
The mystery naked by me,
No narrations to make,
No places to nip out,
No people to niggle and nag!
The words, I cease to string
The thoughts I detest to ink…
Won't even scribble
And scribe for you now!
Let the blank
Be scrubbed smooth,
Stretched very tight too…
I won't serve you anymore,
I am now adamant,
I retire to write.
**We Never Sleep**

We never sleep…
Neither She
Nor I.
Our Heart weeps
A Loud! Cry…
The Past,
We left,
The Present
We live,
The future
Seems very grim…
Gripped by fear,
Grizzled too!
Desolated,
We walk,
Tired,
We run.
We never sleep
Neither she nor I.

# Arish Dhawan

Arish Dhawan is a graduate in Mechanical Engineering and originally hails from Bathinda. A poet by birth and blogger by chance who meant to stumble upon a website named Blogger.com and that changed the way of his life forever. Arish has been a part of 4 anthologies (both national and international) so far. An ardent blogger at www.preciousglories.blogspot.com

He could also be reached at arish.dhawan92@yahoo.com

# My Son Peshawar

I take the pills that make my heart stronger
Swallowing it with a heavy gulp even after years
I watch over my son with a rather strange question
in his mind
Asking if he was a disgrace, as we had no other
child after him.
He was the most absolved of all kids
Playing with sand even at 15; and so I said he was
all I had
But convinced he was none and wanted an
explanation
Of what a pearl means to an oyster.

The other day, he said he wanted a new outfit
That maybe then people will switch their paradigm
So honest my son is how I tell him
That his fingerprints still tap on my skin
Everywhere his cold hands touched.
That deluged the thought of stained clothes and
patches
A grief I had felt before and with same intensity
And I'll keep rinsing until Mushin is achieved
Searching for an ocean that brings back the season
And I place a rose in the barrel of every gun

That I have come across ever since
For my elder kids killed the younger ones
And in that brutality, I lost my son Peshawar

I'm not angry, rather shattered; speechless
For in either way the loss was mine
The world transformed into a language I never
wanted
While resent and gore are all that ever chime
For my elder kids killed the younger ones
And in that brutality, I lost my son Peshawar

☐

## Compassion Will Prevail

You're not what I was meant to be
For I'm not what I should have been.
A hand, a shoulder, an adhesive
Or even a blemished path to the finish line.

Compassion is what I'm
Compassion is what predefines me
For, I'm a paltry of oblivion, you didn't want to be
I'm your footmarks
Those are there to stay long after you're gone.
I'll shed my tears every time you're sad
Worrying for the times you fall flat
Neither are you what you always wanted to be
Nor am I what others expected of me
For I'm a human, and Compassion starts with me.

We do belong somewhere
Maybe a place, a city, or a nation
Or maybe a planet yet to be discovered
But what if we were already where we belonged
'TO EACH OTHER'

# Elora Rath

Apart from being a writer and poet at heart, Elora Rath juggles her life between preparation for PhD and job search simultaneously. Hailing from the small township of Dhenkanal, she finds herself in the temple city Bhubaneswar for the heck of a successful career with her family by her side. She comprehends her innate urge and creative passion towards writing is solely inherited from her mother who rejoiced liberal arts as a medium of expression of her soul. Apart from writing prose and poetry in English, Hindi and Oriya to pen down her bleak emotions on a blank sheet, she also has a keen interest of indulging herself in dancing, singing, photography, travelling, and internet surfing and cooking in her free time. She believes life taught her more than what she could have ever learnt from a very tender age and the reflections of which can be traced in her writing which picks up delicate issues and small charms of human relationships as a core concern. A real life modern relationship article of hers has been featured in the book called "21 Things about Romance" by Grapevine India Publisher. A fictional story from her pen is featured in the book named "Fusion: A mingled flavour mocktail" by Dream House Publication. She has contributed and got selected to be part of 17 other anthologies by now. Being an avid reader and an ardent fan of Cricket, WWE, Romantic Comedies and bollywood masala movies, she finds herself incriminated in any of the above mentioned guilty pleasures when she gets a break from her favourite activities besides work.

# The Journey called Life

A lone soul in retrospection
Looked back at the pathway
On which life leisurely strolled
Leaving its manifest foot prints
To the gold dusted avenue
In the secluded place where
A ravaged orchard and
A shrivelled fountain
Welcomed her essence
To evening skyline
Through the mangled window
Of the vintage-old manor's
Disfigured walls and
Timeworn murals
Made her see through the
Broken pieces of mirrors
Lying on the paved floor
Reminiscing its journey
Romancing with fate
And
Camouflaging the despair!

Odyssey through the pieces
Of speculum scattered below

Flew in a course of time travel
To some land unknown
Resembling a hefty mansion
Decked with variant artefacts
And glistening chandeliers
Emanating aura of divinity
Where a naivety sauntered
In the curved stairs of hallway
Her anklets carelessly danced
Trilling tales of marvel
Her timid azure eyes
Oomph-ed rills of love
Her innocent face
Resembled harmonious dove!

Time vamoosed
As if spirits in thin air
Life consumed bit by bit
Love pinched cheeks
And left her pined for more
Solicitous years gone by
Loneliness cajoled her
Took her in svelte arms
Attachments succumbed
Strings severed and perished
Still the unknown wait

Kept her in unfulfilled spirit
Roaming in the lowland
In eternal tears and strife
Is it the savaged form of?
The journey called life?

## "The pain that was penned!"

As that momentous evening appeared to be still
My shattered solemn heart denied to fly at its will
The blank pages of my notebook flipped in the gush
of air
My flitting unhinged mind does not seem to care!

Life has never been a derailing journey of such upset
days
Your hurting words probe to bind me in a lifelong
cage
Essence of our togetherness always prevailed
Your retreat left me alone and dishevelled!

Tears kissed my cheeks and flowed down in ease
Your displeased face came across and seized
I could not tickle you, to make you smile
Believing that you are far away, took me a while!

Still the hopes in my heart refuse to die
Disconnected from the world, I chose to cry
My cocooned thoughts on flimsy, scribbled to the
end
With my wretched heart, it's the pain that was
penned!

# <u>Nikita Goel</u>

I am a Writer, Blogger, Reader, Teacher and a Counsellor. I am a hardcore believer of Karma and Law of Attraction. I preach to the World that all the Universe, including stars, sky, planets and moons work for you through your mind."What you think you become "is my way of living Life. I am hopelessly optimistic. I am someone who would be there welcoming the new world when everyone around would be mourning the end .There is an eternal quest about knowing myself. There is a lot I learn about myself from people I meet, books I read and places I visit. I am self- obsessed and God says I am his favourite child. Three words that describe me best would be - Believer, Doer and Keeper.

My Blog "The Enchantress" is about celebration of Life. It's about being yourself and accepting every inch of who you are .It talks about happiness being inside you and God being not at churches. It's about a girl who is reluctant to grow up and how she deals with adults around trying to change her. She is a Misfit, she belongs to nobody. She stares at the sky like it's her home. She years to be somewhere, She belongs to the ANGELS. It's my LIFE through my eyes and I hope to read it to my grandchildren someday.

I have been Blogging since pretty long, may be 4-5 years .It's not about liking / loving for me. Writing is to me what Breathing is to you. I write because If I don't I would die. I often feel an urge to write when I am sitting with friends or dreaming at midnight or having lunch at a fine restaurant. It comes anytime and every time to me. It's a way of worshipping God.

# If I'm talking to you

If I'm talking to you
Just look into my eyes
You'll hear what I'd never say

If I'm talking to you
Say you understand
Even if you don't understand

If I'm talking to you
Know that you're special
Seldom are my secrets shared

If I'm talking to you
Kiss my forehead
And tell me you love me

If I'm talking to you
Let me weep as long as I please
Seldom Do I let tears flow

If I'm talking to you
Take my hand to your heart
And Let me feel the Love

If I'm talking to you
Know that I'm hurt
Listen to me all night

If I'm talking to you
I just need to be heard
And pain would be gone

If I'm talking to you
Just look into my eyes
You'll hear what I'd never say

☐

## It isn't all...

It isn't all,
It can't be,
Was it all I wanted?
Why do not I smile?

I can't move,
I feel restrained,
I stand still,
Let me go away.

I am hurt,
I am cheated,
I feel ditched,
Why am I in prison?

Was I wrong?
Should I regret?
Should I forget?
Take me out of it.

I can't share,
I do not speak,
I can't go back,
I do not intend to go.

## Love letters that I'll never sent

Dear,
I have been suffering
I have been hiding from you
How I feel about that

I have been telling myself
"It's gonna fade with time"
"It's gonna fade with time"
It was not what I deserved

That was the last thing
I could expect from you!
I used to boast of you
You were something
That I always felt proud of

I still do...I am proud of you
But the scars remain
No matter how many times
I heal my pain

It was meant to happen that way
I agree...Lord can never be wrong

Things had to be done that way
But all that was only my RIGHT

And as things remain unsaid
Between us, I am left free
To imagine all the crap by myself
And torture myself as much as
I am capable of

And I know
It was nothing for you
But it's a lot for me
But it's a lot for me

Did you ever miss me those days?
Did you realize it would bleed my soul?
Did you find it easier to do all that?
Did you think of me?

I could have gone wrong too,
I keep analyzing, where I did,
But was it not the worst punishment
Was it not too much to bear?

I understand you have suffered too
I know it hurts more there

I have sealed my lips forever
Not to hurt you ever

□

# Memories

Wish I could erase my memories from your mind,
I know how much they pinch you and me.
We need to move on and write new chapters,
Do not hurt me anymore, I beg of you.

I cannot come back as I have moved far away,
Things have changed for us forever.
I know what I did to you is unfair,
But you made my heart bleed.

I can remember all the times you hurt me,
You remind me those which pinch my soul.
I still do not hold any grudges for the past
My love will cherish forever and ever.

I want to feel happiness apart from you,
My life has changed.
I have to reach a new destination,
Be with me as my strength, do not make me weak.

You have forgotten the times, you asked me to leave,
The only thing you remember is I left you
You only told me, Life goes on,
Then why don't you let it go.

Things cannot be same again,
Glass once broken can't be reframed.
Let it show the tiny cracks,
Then break into thousand pieces.

Memories would always make me smile,
Let them not erode with pain.
Our relation can still grow on,
Fruits would never be born.

Like a huge tree, I would be your shelter,
I would protect you from sunrays.
Everything is same. Though everything has changed,
You are there and so am I....

☐

# Writing is a struggle against silence

When I listen to silence
It screams aloud
I often speak in my numbness
Hear me in my warm breaths
Feel my words in my touch
Look into my eyes and let them
Carry the conversation forward
Sometimes Silence makes you lonelier
And there are times it takes you to solitude
Peace, undying peace inside
Those who speak less, listen more
And as they listen more, they know more
Quiet people mostly turn to writers
When writers speak, gems are created
Silence is an ocean...It has its own world
Undiscovered and Unravelled
It's like ripples in the pond
When you throw stones in water
It reaches horizon but shall come back
And join the ocean
Silence is best words said ever!
Silence is best words said ever!!

# Neha Rautela

Her poems have appeared in International anthologies and Journals.

'In Our Own Words' , 'The Art of Being Human Volume 4 -An Anthology of International Poetry' publications of Brian Wrixon  Books (Canada),  PEN International Austria's book on  Malala  , Lovelets – by Butterfly & The Bee and All About Books Global, India , Persona by IIM -C , Synthesis- duet poetry by Poiesis ,Zest of Inklings,    Harvest of New Millennium to name a few.

She truly believes that art is cathartic and loves to indulge in colours. She is a dog lover and stands for being kind to animals.

# Sweet fancy

I imagine you kiss me
Bring love rush to start
I dream of that moment
All days and nights we are apart

When will you come?
What will you say?
Thoughts cross my mind
Sweet fancy's play

Oh! Yes very human
To value what makes us wait
Much like a household rat
Stuck in love's bait!

☐

## Lasting love

They think me a fool,
But I've tried all other ways
That boast of giving joy
& found them all,
Incomplete

Ugly half- headed happiness
Trying in vain,
To console a cracked heart

But your love is intense
Even violent,
Makes me powerless
And stirs my entire being

Sometimes it's just scary
To heart what you mean
God knows if this is madness
Or lasting love!

## Debdip Maitra

Debdip Maitra is just another middle class boy
currently pursuing B.Tech in Mechanical
Engineering. A hopeless romantic, he believes in
being down to earth, and letting his words & actions
do the talking. A passionate quizzer, he also loves
reading, and can hardly spend a day without music.
Basically laid back by nature, you'll nevertheless
find him quite vocal about the things he is
passionate about!

# Refuse To Abandon Hope Still

And that eye, beauty divine,
Takes me to places unknown.
Intoxication, that potent wine,
Of that face, on me has grown.

Sail through the storm ravaged seas,
Or hike through the forest.
For the merest chance of a kiss,
I am ready to court the arrest,

Of that free bird, my heart...
I could throw away all my wealth,
For that divine touch of art.
Her face, that through subtle stealth,

Has robbed me of my sanity...
Thus here I fly, the bug to fire,
Attraction, in all its fatality,
A slave to this mad desire...

Will my heart be warmed?
Or my house be burnt to a cinder?
As I rush on disarmed,
My mind does wonder...

Will she rush to me with a sniff?
Or with a smile of evil allure,
Push me off the precipitous cliff?
Doesn't matter, her call's allure,

Has me rushing blindly once more.
Call me a fool if you will,
But for a key to that golden door,
I refuse to abandon hope still...

☐

# The Strength of Friendship

The soul lives there in the silent breath,
And the heart wanders in search of its wealth.
Weary I cry, but still totter on,
My feet may bleed, but the mind races on.

Shattered dreams, blood stained on the floor,
Broken pieces, and frustration I roar.
Seeking escape, I pound on the walls,
My heart's cry, on deaf ears it falls.

Disjoint images, flash through my mind,
Back through time, my memory rewinds.
Again I stand, beneath that willow,
The incessant tears, again I swallow.

Hurt and alone, as I sat there crying,
You were the only one who came prying.
You extended your hand, and flashed a smile,
All my worries seemed to vanish for a while.

With you standing by me, I accepted my difference,
You showed me the beauty, among the forests
dense.
That darkness paves the way, for the stars to shine,

And laugh the world may, my identity was mine.

Now as I'm entombed, once more by my fright,
And situation's chains wrap around me so tight.
Your face burns bright, the bonds of our friendship,
Lends me yet again, the strength to face the
hardships.

And as I run once more, drenching myself in the
rain,
The cold drops on my skin, wash away the pain.
And I sense you beside me, hiding in the trees,
I now feel secure; my heart finally knows peace...

# Jyoti Jain

Jyoti Jain, born and brought up in Rajasthan. She graduated in biology but at her graduation she felt that science wasn't for her. She found her true calling in writing so she converted her hobby into a profession. Our amateur and wonderful writer is pursuing her P.G. in journalism and mass communication. She is also a writer at surabhi publications.

## I wish...

I wish,
I have some connections to you again.
My life with you anonymously again.
Grievance may become a thing of the past again.
Our all meetings will be the first meeting again.
Created a new trail in the streets with you again.
Every drop of your love be mine again.
And my soul lost herself in you again.
I just wish,
Your smile will be my race again.

□

## Who is yours?

Who is yours after me? He asked.
The blue sky- she said.
Besides the blue sky.
Who is yours?? He asked.
Green paddy- she said.
Apart grains who is yours? He asked.
The hazel river- she said.
After river?? He asked.
The dusty evening- she said.
Except those evenings? He asked.
The thundering storm- she said.
Beyond storms?? He asked.
The black soil- she said.
After black soil?? Sadly he demand.
You are the one, who is mine.
After the life, in the divine.
She cheers up.

# <u>Sunayna Pal</u>

Sunayna Pal, born and brought up in Mumbai, shifted to USA for a little while after her marriage but misses Mumbai terribly and awaits her return. She has PG degrees from XLRI and Annamalai University and worked in the Corporate World for five odd years but quit it in 2009 and embarked on her heart's pursuits.

She started "Art with Sunayna" (artwithsunayna.wordpress.com) to teach and sell art for NGOs. She is also a certified graphologist (sos4graphology.com) who helps everyone to understand themselves better by using a mix of graphotherapy, healing and affirmations and corporate to hire better.

In midst of all this and being a home maker, gardener and photographer, she also finds the time to write. She loves to write from her daily life experiences. Sunayna was the Mumbai reporter for Evergreen Magazine. Many of her articles have been published in TOI, New woman, Women's era and she is a proud contributor at many other e-magazines and sites and the anthology "Mighty Thoughts" and "The second Life." and is eagerly awaiting few other publications.

In her little spare time, she also maintains a blog at mannkiwindow.wordpress.com and can be contacted at sunayna.pal@gmail.com. She is currently writing a fictional story slightly inspired by her experience in the USA.

# The waiting room

I came in the room crying
With shock of the sublime.
The doctor would meet me
When he thought it was the ideal time.

As I grew up,
I understood where I was
It wasn't really a bad place,
More like a play between the pause.
I met many a nice people
Waiting with me here
Since I had the time,
I exchanged smiles and tears.

Not all whom I met were kind
Elders told me to try heal their tear.
I saw many people leave me
As the doctor called them near.

I liked one person in particular
I spent most of my time with him,
Together, we added a few new members
But the chances of meeting the doctor were still slim.
Finally came my turn and as surprised as I could be

I already felt pretty healed
And didn't quite want to go
But everyone must as destined.

## Heaven

What is this place of my dreams?
Where loved ones meet me
Where angels bless me
Where god comes home.

Where is this place of my dreams?
Where I eagerly wait to go
Where my heart finds rest.
Which makes me sad while leaving?

Who knows of this place of my dreams?
How do I go there often?

# Mahua Sen

Mahua Sen was born in Bihar and grew up in New Delhi. She is the second daughter of Dr. SM Chowdhury and Mrs. Krishna Chowdhury.

Mahua is a Post-graduate in Journalism and worked as a Journalist and a Banker. She is the author of a poetry book named 'Insights', published under the flagship of Authorspress, which received much appreciation. She is also a freelance writer and contributing author of many books. She used to play with alliteration and metaphors ever since a tender age. She is an avid reader and a music-lover. She believes in the simple joys of life.

Mahua lives in Hyderabad with her husband, Utpal Sen and her four-year old child Raunav Sen whom she calls her 'Sunshine'.

To know more about Mahua Sen, mail her at sen.mahua5@gmail.com

# Mother, My Love...!!!

Your crimson love warms my soul,
Your caring ways soothes me, bliss you dole!
Your tender hug annihilate my agony,
Rhymes my heart with sweet cacophony!

You spruce up my life with purple hues,
Mother, you take me out of all my blues!!
Bearing all whimpers and cleaning my drool,
Enriching my life and you never lost your cool!

You showed me light in times of foreboding,
Bore all stress with smile endearing!
Fed me, clothed me, gave me all luxury,
Wiped my tears, brought me smile with your
buffoonery!

I can never thank you enough for all that you've
done,
When I skinned my knees and skinned my heart,
You picked me up and healed my scar,
Mother, you are my love and the guiding star!!

# Ethereal Love...!

The memoirs of love,
Hovering in my mind like dove!
Hammering a hole in my heart,
Reminiscing bygone and tears blot!

For you were the antidote to my misery,
You painted my soul with your love, like ivory!
You showed me the rainbow amidst the cloud,
For you were a blessing in disguise from God!

Your tender touch was so pure,
Played a sublime symphony in heart' s core!
Your resplendent eyes gave me hope,
And arduous struggle I could cope!!

The conjuring passion that you dole,
Cascading memories warm my soul!
Milieu of love I'd wrap around,
Until my ashes daub into the ground!!